DANGEROUS SERPENT'S SECRET DESIRE

COMPANY 417 SHIFTERS SERIES

AMELIA WILSON

CHAPTER ONE

Gwen

I don't get upset when my alarm rings. I just roll from the bed without thinking much about things at all. The breeze from the air conditioning vent passes over my naked body and sends goosebumps all over me. I don't react to that either. I pad my way past my dresser and step into the bathroom. I walk directly to the shower and slide open the glass door so I can enter. I close it and turn the water on. The water is cold as it sprays over me. I don't get irritated. I don't feel anything. I just move the temperature control lever to the left and the water gradually warms.

Autopilot.

That's my life.

I wake up and walk to the bathroom and I shower. I don't think. I don't react. I don't feel.

I don't get upset when my alarm rings because I don't get upset at all.

The water grows warm and I wash my hair without thinking about the pleasantness of the scent of the floral ingredients in the shampoo. I run a gently exfoliating cloth over my body and the tea tree oil soap fills the shower with a lovely woodsy smell that also does nothing for me at all. I rinse off and then take the showerhead from its hook and bring it down between my legs.

The jets of water create an immediate physical effect as my pussy lights up with sensation. I adjust the flow of the showerhead and center the attention on my clit. I do this on autopilot as well. I always masturbate in the shower. It's a habit. It's entirely physical. I don't enjoy it. Oh, I bring myself to orgasm. Some of the orgasms are powerful. When they are, I note what I might have done differently. It's all part of my routine.

I feel nothing.

I haven't felt anything in four years.

If I allow myself to feel, I will certainly disappear into nothing at all.

Oh, I feel the sensations of the jet. I feel the way the water stimulates my pussy and the way my clit throbs and sends pleasure through me. Without consciously noting what feels good or doesn't, I adjust the jets on an ongoing basis to progress toward orgasm. I put one hand on the tiles in front of me to steady myself as I spread my legs slightly to give better access.

When my orgasm comes, my body tenses up and I

can feel my abdomen clenching with the climax. Then, it releases and pleasure washes over me as I keep the jet focused. The pleasure pulses powerfully through me and when my pussy grows too sensitive, I lift the jet away and put it back on the hook. I rinse off. Then, I turn the water off and step out. I dry myself and wrap myself in a terrycloth robe. I step into my slippers and then walk back into my room and then out my door. The shower and masturbation are checked off my mental list and the next item to address is coffee.

I reach the kitchen and select a coffee mug. It has a picture of a cat from a famous comic strip with his catch-phrase encapsulated in a cartoonish speech bubble. I set it on the counter and add water to the reservoir of the small drip coffee maker I took home when the office switched to one of those new single-cup machines.

I place a single paper filter in the basket of the machine and carefully spoon four tablespoons of coffee grounds into the filter. I tap the basket lightly to settle the grounds, then close the machine and start the brew cycle.

While the coffee brews, I add a tablespoon of butter to a frying pan and set the burner to medium heat. When the butter is melted, I crack two eggs into the pan. A drop of oil splashes onto my thigh and leaves a small red mark. The mark burns but I don't react to it other than wipe the oil off with a paper towel. I make a mental note to dress before breakfast from now on.

While the eggs fry, I place a slice of bread in the toaster and slice an orange. The coffeemaker chimes to let me know the coffee is ready. I flip my eggs and pour a cup of coffee. I measure a teaspoon of sugar into the coffee and add enough cream to turn the liquid a golden-brown color. I use a turner to remove the eggs from the frying pan and set them on my plate next to the oranges. The toaster pops and I spread an even layer of jam over it before placing it on the plate. I take the food and the coffee to the dining room and eat slowly, methodically, sipping my coffee after every third bite.

The eggs are perfectly over-easy, as always. The coffee is perfectly sweetened so the bitterness of the roast is still evident behind the sugar and the cream. The toast is crisped a rich brown with just enough jam to be sweet but not cloying.

It's a good breakfast, like every breakfast for the past four years and I eat it slowly and methodically as I've eaten every breakfast for the past four years.

When breakfast is finished, I rinse my dishes and set them in the dishwasher then return to my room to dress. I wear panties that, while attractive and well-fitted, are intended to be comfortable, not sexy. I select a bra designed in a similar fashion. All of my underwear is similar in that regard. I've never bothered to buy sexy clothing. Since I don't intend to feel an emotional connection to anyone and my physical needs are served well enough by my daily shower, there's no need to look sexy for anyone.

I wear a white button-down blouse and a dark grey skirt with a matching blazer. The skirt hangs well below my knee and is slitted modestly. The clothing is cut well and becoming to my figure but, like the underwear, is functional, not attention-seeking. In this case, the function is to appear professional but approachable enough that the working-class families I work with won't feel uncomfortable around me.

The shoes—black faux-suede wedges with a closed toe and matte-gold buckles—serve the same function. I'm well-dressed but I don't think I'm better than you. You can trust me.

I gather my phone, purse, wallet, car keys, and briefcase. I set the code to arm the alarm system I installed last year after the father of one of our cases made death threats to several of the employees at my office. The alarm chirps to let me know I have sixty seconds to leave and lock the front door. I make it out with exactly twenty-seven seconds to spare, then head to my car and drive to work.

Just another day to avoid feeling anything. Just like every other day.

CHAPTER TWO

Barrett

A day off.

I need it.

It's fire season, which means work at the station or, more accurately, at various sites of fires, has been overwhelming of late. I love my job and I can't imagine a better group of people than the firefighters at Company 417. There's not one of them I wouldn't trust with my life and I'm certain they feel the same way.

A mountain lion eyes me suspiciously as I cross her path. Of course, she does. She's never seen anything like me. She's certainly seen diamondback rattlesnakes before but she's never seen one about twenty-two feet long and four hundred pounds. She's certainly never seen one that makes her the prey rather than the predator. In fact, she's never seen anything that she'd recognize as a predator when compared to her. So, she just thinks of me as if she might be a bison or a buck too large to fall. I'm not prey for her but I'm also not a threat. I'm just a giant, unknown animal slithering past her.

She's right, too. I have no interest in making her prey.

I don't eat very often as my snake. Snake physiology is substantially different than human physiology. Also, and I think this is almost unique among shifters, there doesn't seem to be a correlation between eating as a snake and receiving the benefits of the meal as a human. I have wolf friends. I have tiger friends. I have friends who are mountain lions. I even have a friend who is a gorilla. If they are full as a human, they are full as an animal. If they eat as a lion or tiger, their human form is full when they shift back.

For snakes, it is just different.

I ate a few months ago as my serpent, a whitetail deer. I'm still full. I will be until several more months pass, unless I remain a serpent for twenty or thirty days straight instead of taking a few hours here and there when I can. As for my human form, I need my three squares a day just like anyone else.

I slide out of the trees and head back to my car. I'm not going to shift back yet. I just want some sun and my car is parked on a rise in a break in the trees and the warmth will be wonderful for me to bask in and enjoy. As I move, I feel a great deal of joy at the thought of the sun on me. That's part of the reptilian nature of my snake brain.

I retain who I am but the emotions and desires are felt far more powerfully.

It doesn't take too long to get where I'm going and as I coil myself and feel the warmth, the effect is about as wonderful as a hot shower on a cold day. I'd sing if I could in this form. I can't, of course, but I content myself with a lazy rattle.

I bask for twenty minutes or so before I decide it's time to head home. My next shift, work shift that is, doesn't start until tomorrow morning, but there's some work I want to do around the house before then, so I don't want to burn all my daylight away.

I shift back into human form and sigh. The sun still feels nice and warm but it's just not the same feeling as it is in my snake form. Perhaps that's a function of the human brain more than it is the human body. Human brains are compulsively analytical. We must know not only what is but *how* it is and *why* it is and *what* might cause it to change. It's an excellent adaptation and probably the primary reason humans are the dominant species on Earth but it makes it difficult to truly enjoy things. To my snake brain, warmth is warmth and warmth is wonderful and there's no need to think any further on the matter.

It occurs to me I'm fortunate. For some reason, reptilian shifters shift completely, clothes and all. We think it has to do with our molting process or something like that. The body is already used to having extra layers, maybe. It's a nice thing to tease other shifters about.

There are a lot of funny stories from the guys at Company 417, the fire station where I work. Most of us are shifters and they have plenty of embarrassing stories about shifting back naked and having to hide from sight.

I drive home with the top rolled down and the feel of the wind in my hair briefly makes me reconsider whether humans are handicapped in their enjoyment of things after all. I think that briefly, very briefly.

Briefly, because after a mile or so, I smell smoke. Another mile and I see the fire. It's about five miles distant and still small but burning rapidly. I quickly call the station and learn that Engine Five is already on its way.

The fire is near the road but not near enough that I feel a need to detour. That is extremely fortunate. If I had detoured, Peanut would have died.

I feel the screaming before I hear it. That's my snake brain. I'm in human form, so I don't exactly have heightened physical sensitivity to vibration but I notice it because I am used to paying attention to such changes.

The rest is muscle memory and a firefighter's instinct. I park the car on the side of the road and run toward the flames. The screaming is louder now and there's no mistaking the high pitch of a small child. I shift into snake form when I reach the fire and slither around the flames. Being low to the ground protects my airways from the smoke but my reptilian circulation is far more sensitive to the heat. I have only a few moments before I will have to shift back to human form.

I flick my tongue out and pick up the child's scent through the smoke. She is close. I find her a few yards away hiding behind a bush that hasn't yet caught fire. I slither as close as possible before shifting back to human form. I shift to human form and approach her. The bush is beginning to smoke when I reach her and I don't have time to talk, so I pick her up and run out of the flame.

I leave the fire just in time to see that fire engine stop on the side of the highway. The child clings desperately to me, still crying and shaking with fear.

"It's all right," I tell her. "You're safe now."

CHAPTER THREE

Gwen

It is another day.

I don't get upset when my alarm rings and roll from the bed without thinking and without reacting to the too-cold air conditioner on my naked body. I walk to the bathroom and into the shower and turn the water on. The cold freezes me and I turn hot without reacting like every other morning of my autopilot life. I shampoo my hair with expensive floral shampoo that doesn't please me. I exfoliate with expensive tea tree oil sop that doesn't please me. I rinse off and use the shower head to masturbate.

I put my hand on the tile to steady myself and I bring myself to orgasm. I rinse off. I turn the water off and step out. I dry myself, put on my robe, get my feet in my slippers and go make coffee. It's every other morning and Gwen the robot successfully avoids giving a damn about anything at all.

Except I don't.

As I sit at my little table with my coffee, I break down and think of the little boy I interviewed yesterday. He has a cast on one leg and one arm and he doesn't know when his mother will wake up from her coma. He's six years old and he doesn't understand why his new daddy did this to them.

His third new daddy this year.

He doesn't know his mother is addicted to heroin. He doesn't know anything about that at all.

And I weep because I believe his only real hope is for his mother never to wake up from her coma so that his mother's younger brother can take him and raise him in his stable home with his wife of fourteen years and his two cousins. The boy is happy there. The boy is often left there for weeks at a time. I want his mother dead.

So, I deal not only with overpowering sympathy for the boy but also with crushing guilt for wishing a woman dead.

For five minutes.

Then, I put my coffee down and walk back to the room and then back to the bathroom, and then into the shower where I wash my hair with floral shampoo, exfoliate with tea tree oil body wash, masturbate with the shower head, rinse off, dry off, put my robe back on, get into my slippers and walk back out.

The emotions are gone.

I don't feel anymore.

I'm back on autopilot now that the system is reset.

I know this is unhealthy. Hell, I'm a psychologist. If a client described to me behavior like mine, I would immediately talk to them about needing to address the situation. I can't go through life like some kind of automaton.

But I must.

I work for the city as a child psychologist. I have no private practice. My duties are for the purposes of investigation and not therapeutic. That means I speak with children to discover what's wrong and to see if that means law enforcement or another agency needs to act.

I don't get to help the children.

I diagnose child after child, but I don't get to help them. The best I can do is get an agency involved if there is a direct threat to the child's physical safety. That happens far less than you might imagine. So, I can choose to feel and let that kill me or I can choose not to feel and avoid living. I choose not to feel because it would be selfish of me to allow my emotions to get in the way of getting children the help they need.

Except the children don't usually get the help they need. Like that little boy. If his mother wakes up—and for some reason, they always manage to wake up—she'll cry and beg and promise to get help and talk about how much she loves her son. She might even pull a thirty-day stint in rehab and come out with her hair done and makeup applied, looking just like a responsible citizen desperate to prove she can be a good mother. Then, she'll go home with her son, get high and fuck another pimp or john who will beat her son again until the kid is either killed or so traumatized, that he becomes a drug addict himself.

And I have to stand idly by and watch that happen.

I close my eyes and take three deep breaths before dressing myself. It helps. Once more, I don't feel anything. That's good. That's safer than feeling despair and anger and desperation and heartbreak.

My phone rings. I stare at it for a moment, temporarily unsure how to respond to a break in my routine. Finally, I pick the phone up. My boss.

"Gwen, thank God you answered. I have a case for you. Fire Department just rescued a kid from a fire. I need you to go to the firefighter's house where she's staying and interview her."

"Why is she at the firefighter's house? Shouldn't we bring her to CPS?"

"She refuses to leave the firefighter that rescued her. Gave PD a lot of trouble when they tried. They were afraid she'd hurt herself. They were going to force her and the fireman intervened, said there was no way in hell they were going to take her until she was calm and secure."

This kind of thing is a common response of children rescued from traumatic situations. The fireman, though, shows impressive care for the victim. That impresses me. "Okay. Send me the address."

I drive to the address: a small but well-put-together ranch house with a beautifully landscaped yard. An SUV is parked in the driveway, covered in ash. I walk to the door wearing the empathetic smile I've perfected over years in this profession.

The firefighter answers the door and for the first time in four years, I'm speechless. He is tall, powerfully built, and handsome but it is his eyes that capture me. They are a deep, liquid green, and seem to stare through me—through the façade of happiness I wear to work, through the façade of emotionlessness I wear at home, through to the real Gwendolyn Anjanette Montgomery that cries and rages in desperation at the children I have to watch suffer every day. He sees me, and I can't recall the last time anyone has.

The most recent child is in this godlike man's arms, holding him like a life preserver. She stares mistrustfully at me and I remember myself. I smile widely and offer my hand. "Hi! I'm Gwen. What's your name?"

She doesn't answer but clings more tightly to the firefighter. He takes my offered hand. "Hi Gwen, I'm Barrett. Will you come inside?" To the girl, he says, "Peanut, I promise you. She's not going to try to take you away unless you want to go with her."

"Let's go talk, Sweetie," I say.

As soon as he tries to put her down, she screams and kicks and clings to him. I tell Barrett, "It's okay. We can talk later." To the girl, I ask, "Your name is Peanut?"

"She doesn't talk," Barret replies. "I don't think it's because she can't. She just won't. So, I couldn't get her name from her so I call her Peanut."

"Why Peanut?" I ask.

He shrugs and I think I catch a slight smile on the girl's face as the shrug lifts her up a bit. "She's tiny and perfect, like a peanut."

It's a strangely adorable answer. Later, after Peanut is fast asleep and I'm experiencing my first orgasm in four years that didn't come from a shower head, I tell myself his adorable answer is why I sleep with him. That's not the real reason, though. His green eyes are hypnotic and any girl would count herself lucky to look into them as her legs shake underneath the man but that's not why I sleep with him either.

I sleep with him because he saw the real me and I thought the real me was gone a long time ago. I sleep with him because I am still Gwendolyn Anjanette Montgomery after all and I feel like everything is going to be okay. It's been four years since I've felt that way.

CHAPTER FOUR

Barrett

It's a big mistake.

That's the first thing that crosses my mind.

Gwen is my very first time with a woman. Okay, that isn't the whole picture. Gwen is my first time with a woman who isn't also a shifter. This is a big mistake.

The mistake is compounded by something, too. It is compounded by the fact that she doesn't know that I'm a shifter.

So, the first mistake is sleeping with a woman who's straight human. Not orientation. I just mean fully human and no shifter. Relationships just don't work out with straight humans. At least, most of the time they don't. The second mistake is sleeping with her before I take the time to tell her about my serpent. It's a bad idea.

Sex with pure humans isn't unwise. The only time it

is unwise is when it's more than sex. I don't even mean that in a romantic sense. I mean there is no way we won't see each other constantly. If for some reason I meet a girl at a bar and we end up in bed together, a one-night stand, it's fine. The complications of a shifter/non-shifter relationship don't come into play. That kind of thing is a different story altogether.

But there is always the potential for a baby. Shifter mothers have shifter babies one hundred percent of the time. Human mothers with a shifter partner have shifter babies about seventy-five percent of the time. Protections fail. It's part of life, protections failing.

So, if I need companionship, I go to a shifter bar to try my luck.

And yet here I am with this girl next to me and that makes me stupid.

But I want her again.

That makes *stupid* closer to *completely fucking insane*.

The forests away from the city, the ones I frequent when I want to go wild, are filled with melliferous flowers. That's a fancy term for flowers that tend to attract bees that produce a great deal of honey with them. That's like Gwen. She's next to me and it feels like she's a honey-yielding flower. She's beautiful but what makes her amazing is how she somehow gives something of herself to me and it fills me with...

Okay, I'm not a poet. The point is, if I were a bee, she is the exact kind of flower that would attract me and I would end up with a lot of honey. In this case, I'm attracted to her and I'm ending up with a great many emotions I don't usually feel. The emotions are wonderful even if they're also troubling. I gently roll from the bed, throw on a robe, and make my way to the guest bedroom where I've put Peanut.

She's sleeping peacefully, which is a pretty dramatic blessing considering everything she's endured. Asleep, with the fear and shock of the day before gone from her face, she seems so small. Of course, she seemed small even with all of the fear but now she seems small in a beautiful way, just a normal kid living her life. I wonder who she is and when the trauma from the fire will dissipate so she can go back to being whoever she is.

I make my way back to my bedroom and then into the master bathroom. A few seconds later, I'm enjoying the heat of the water and it drives away a lot of the lingering stress. The curtain pulls open and Gwen steps in. What stress the water doesn't drive away, Gwen does.

After, we dress silently. Gwen's face betrays no emotion. She's an enigma. No doubt that's part of what attracts me to her. She makes love like a woman who's just reunited with her lover after years apart but when we're not having sex, she is quiet and reserved and almost clinical in her behavior. I want to know what's behind that veneer. I've never been so interested in getting to know a woman beyond what she likes in the bedroom before.

I finish dressing just as the door to the bedroom opens and Peanut shuffles in. She rubs sleep from her eyes and for the briefest of moments, Gwen's face softens, confirming what I suspected earlier, that she is a caring and kindhearted person.

"Good morning!" Gwen says brightly, smiling at Peanut. Peanut ignores her and walks to me, holding her arms up for me to pick her up. I do and she leans her head on my chest and stares suspiciously at Gwen.

Gwen continues to smile at her. "Is it okay if I talk with you?"

Peanut doesn't respond, so I ask, "Peanut, Miss Gwen is here to help us. Would you mind talking to her a little so she can know how to help us?"

Peanut nods but doesn't say anything.

Gwen beams. "First, what's your name?"

Peanut remains silent.

"How old are you, Peanut?"

Still silent.

Gwen holds up four fingers. "Are you this old?"

No response.

Five fingers. "This much?"

No response.

"Peanut, will you answer Miss Gwen, please?"

"That's okay," Gwen interrupts quickly. "We can get to that later." She flips her hand nonchalantly to let Peanut know it's no big deal, then turns to her and asks, "Peanut, are you hurt anywhere on your body?"

Peanut nods and gestures to her chest and back and legs.

"Poor baby," Gwen says. "Can you tell me what happened?"

Peanut doesn't answer.

Gwen reaches for her. "Do you mind if I look?"

Peanut shrieks and shies away from Gwen. I'm not prepared for the violence of her reaction and I stumble a little. Gwen quickly pulls away, "That's okay. We'll talk when you're ready."

"Peanut," I coax. "Miss Gwen is a really nice lady and she's trying to help. Can you please talk to her?"

"No hurry," Gwen quickly says, "But do you mind if I talk to Mr. Barrett for a moment?"

Peanut thinks a moment, then nods. We walk out to the living room. I set her down and she trots over to the couch. I don't know if she expects it but I put on some cartoons for her. She doesn't react to the animated antics but watches with rapt attention. I gesture with my head and then step into the kitchen and Gwen follows.

"It's important we don't force her to talk," Gwen says right away. "Children who have experienced shock are often slow to open up. We'll keep trying but don't get anxious if it takes her a while to respond. The most important thing we can do for her right now is to help her feel safe. Right now, that means being within twenty feet of you at all times and not talking to anyone and that's okay. We build the trust first, then we talk. Think of now as crawling and talking will be walking."

God, this woman is amazing.

"I am on active duty right now," I say, "but that active

duty is at present keeping watch over Peanut so there's no issue with that. I mean, how the city will survive without its greatest firefighter, I don't know, but that's the status."

She smiles and says, "We'll just have to pray nobody plays with matches." As though she realizes she smiles, her face goes impassive again. "I have one job right now, too," she says, "and I'm going to check in with the office and then go home to pack a bag. Until we get her to open up, I'll need to stay here while I evaluate her case. If that's okay."

"Fine with me," I say. I know that likely means more sex and I'm not upset about that at all but I'm more excited to get to know Gwen than I am to fuck her.

Okay, I'm a man. I'm at least the same amount of excited to get to know her. Well, maybe it's sixty-forty in favor of the sex but for Christ's sake, this woman has a perfect body and is very, very skilled in the bedroom. I can be forgiven.

I make up a guest room even as I hope Gwen won't use it. It occurs to me that I'm in a lot of trouble with her. I've already gone too far. Right or wrong, I want more than a one-night stand from her. How much exactly I want, I'm not sure, but I know I want more than just her body.

This is so stupid.

That won't stop me, though.

CHAPTER FIVE

Gwen

There are at least eight thousand reasons this is stupid.

I don't give a damn.

Even if somehow my brain wires itself correctly again, reset or something so I can think through all of those eight thousand reasons, I still won't stop.

I can't.

For the first time in longer than I can remember, I want something other than an end to the pain of my life. I want something other than to be able to numb myself to everything I face on a daily basis.

I want Barrett.

I want him and I want him desperately.

I don't know if it is Barrett who breaks through the numbness and makes me vulnerable, who somehow drives away my ability, or even my desire to let down all the shields I put up to protect myself from all the sadness and horror I see. It could be him but there could also be something in that little girl. She clings to him as her rescuer and maybe it is simply her need for a rescuer, emotionally I mean, that makes her different from the others.

No, that's bullshit.

She's not different from the others in terms of her need. There is something about her that draws me, though. I don't know what it is other than I see in her eyes a brightness she hasn't lost yet and that brightness is something powerful, desperately powerful. Maybe she draws me to her because I need to find a way to keep that brightness from disappearing, from turning into the dull, hopeless emptiness I see in so many of the children my job puts before me.

And in myself, too, I guess.

I am really setting myself up to be hurt. That's the thing about this situation I can't escape. That's the thing I need to consider, for Christ's sake. After only two days my emotions are back in force and my desires are far too strong for the situation. Hell, they would be too strong if I weren't behaving like a robot just forty-eight hours ago. I don't know what it is about Barrett that does this to me. I know, though, that I'm walking a tightrope and if I plunge over one side or the other, I might never be able to come back.

The smart thing for me to do is walk away right now.

I get up from the bed and walk out of the room. I am

not walking away, the thing I just decided is the smart course of action. Hell no. Smart isn't on my agenda. Instead, I walk directly toward what I really must walk away from. I get to Barrett's bedroom door and crack it open. "Are you awake?" I ask. It's a stupid question because if he is not awake, I intend to wake him up.

"Sure, come in," He replies. I step inside and close the door behind me. He reclines on the bed, a book in his hand. I can't make out the title. He wears only lounge pajama bottoms, deep green. The only light is the lamp next to him on the nightstand but I still imagine I see the green of his eyes somehow intensified with the green of the cotton trousers.

He sets the book down. "Is everything okay?"

For the first time in years, I'm being honest when I say, "It is." Oh, what's okay is very limited in scope but it's still the truth.

I wear only my robe. It's gauzy and delicate but in the dim light, it might as well be a thick woolen dress. It doesn't matter anyway. I do not need it for now. I walk to the side of the bed across from him and stare at his face as I undo the tie holding the robe in place. It opens and I feel a thrill as those emerald eyes strain to see what shadows must be mostly. I run my hands up the inside of the robe and then push it over my shoulders so it falls to the floor and leaves me naked. Then, I climb onto the bed and his eyes widen as he realizes what's going to happen. He reaches for me but I gently take hold of his hands and push them to the side. I will let him take me but first I want to make him feel good. That's another first for me.

I kiss him deeply and passionately, still holding his hands down. After a few seconds, I let my mouth travel down his neck to his chest. I suckle first one nipple then the other. This is the first time I ever did that, lingering on a man's nipple. I don't know why I do it other than I'm not a robot right now and the point of this moment isn't empty culmination. I can tell Barrett likes it. He stiffens and groans as I suck and move my tongue.

His body responds in other ways, too. I feel his cock beneath his cotton bottoms. It grows and presses against me. My pussy convulses slightly at the feeling but I resist the urge to satisfy myself at the moment. I want to satisfy him, and that desire feels beautiful. I move back and forth between his nipples, briefly, and then kiss his breastbone before I let my mouth travel down his navel. I release his hands and pull his pants down. I place my lips on the tip of his cock, then slide my tongue down his shaft as far as it will go. I hold that position and lower my mouth over his cock until my lips press against the base of his shaft, then suck all the way back up to the tip, twisting my head and circling my tongue around his cock.

He groans and I can tell he's already close. I keep going at a steady pace. When he is about to cum, he tries to pull me off but I hold his hands down and drop my head until my lips are pressed hard against his shaft. I use my tongue to massage his balls while he cums. I feel his cock pulse hard in my throat and swallow in time to the pulses.

I don't stop until his cock stops twitching. I pull off of him and he is still hard. "Now you can fuck me," I say.

He moves, so quickly I am almost frightened. Before I know it, I'm on my back with my legs open. When he slams into me, I gasp. The façade falls and I am naked before him, in mind as well as the body.

"Oh my God," I breathe as he slams hard into me. My toes curl and warmth pools in my belly. Just before I cum, he places a hand on me just above my pussy and says, "Wait."

I don't know how but my body somehow manages to heed that command even though the sensations I feel are already greater than every orgasm I've ever experienced. He begins to gently graze the tip of his thumb over my clit. I stiffen and my eyes and mouth fly open wide and again he says, "Wait."

I feel my orgasm build deep inside me until it is a solid ball of pleasure just above and behind my clit. My pussy shivers and struggles to hold back the flood while his cock continues to massage my g-spot and his thumb continues to wind my clit up to the breaking point.

My whole body begins to twitch but it's not until he says, "Cum for me, Gwen," that I finally orgasm.

The ball of pleasure in my stomach bursts, then reforms and bursts again, over and over and over. I burst and reform with it, screaming and shaking and moaning as my entire body is wracked with the sensation.

For a beautiful moment, all the pain and fear and hurt and grief I've buried is gone. There is only Barrett and I and I am completely, beautifully, exquisitely his.

Then his orgasm joins mine. My body, somehow sensing his climax, instantly tightens and seems to pull him deeper inside.

Finally, we collapse with exhaustion, breathing heavily as our bodies reach the final throes of coupling and settle down to bask in the afterglow.

I'm no longer numb.

CHAPTER SIX

Barrett

We sit at my dining room table and I set a plate of spaghetti in front of Gwen. She looks at me with a smile and I don't know if it's gratitude or if maybe she's just impressed with my world-famous meat sauce. Okay, it's more like *famous at the fire station* but until Gwen and Peanut, the fire station is pretty much my whole world so I'm not backing down from what I call it. I smile back at her and put the platter of garlic bread down on the table.

I put a smaller plate of spaghetti in front of Peanut and smile at her, too. Peanut says, "Thank you."

I say, "You're welcome, Peanut," and then, of course, stare in shock at her. I look at Gwen. She looks at Peanut in shock as well. I slide my chair closer to the little girl and say, "You... you speak English." She nods cautiously and I say, "We didn't know, honey. We didn't know anything about you." She presses her lips together nervously. I sit down and smile. "I'm glad you speak English because that means I can talk to you and you can talk to us, too."

She nods slowly. Gwen says, "and I can talk to you, too. Is that okay?"

She turns to Gwen and nods slowly again. Gwen smiles and says, "Can you tell me your name, sweetie?"

The girl says softly, "I like Peanut."

Gwen smiles and says, "I like Peanut, too. My name is Gwen."

Peanut nods and then looks at me. "And you're Barrett."

"That's right," I say.

"Peanut?" Gwen asks. The girl turns to her and Gwen says, "I like calling you Peanut and I'm really glad you like it but we need to know if you have another name, a name that people called you before Barrett called you Peanut."

She looks down at the table and says, "I'm not allowed to say that name."

"Why aren't you allowed?" Gwen asks. "Who told you that you couldn't say that name?"

"I'm hungry," Peanut says. "Can I eat now?"

"Sure, Sweetie," I say. I move my chair back. I look at Gwen, hoping she won't be irritated that I let Peanut end the conversation. Gwen smiles at me, though, and it not only reassures me but makes me feel pretty damned good about things. God, I really am falling for this woman. If Peanut wasn't a far bigger priority than the complications that brings to my life, I might dwell on it.

Gwen takes a bite of her spaghetti and says, "Mmm-mmm! Oh, wow. This spaghetti is really good!" She says it almost like a cartoon character. She's exaggerating for Peanut's benefit, of course, but it works.

Peanut takes a bite and says, "Mmmmmm! Really good spaghetti!" There is actual enthusiasm in her voice, and that thrills me.

I smile, take a bite, and say, "Mmmmmmm! I made this spaghetti!" Peanut giggles and the sound is the first unreservedly happy sound that little girl has made since I pulled her away from the fire. It's a profound moment and if not for my pretty substantial male ego (and that goes for the human as well as serpent ego) keeping me from showing the emotion, I might let some tears roll down my cheeks.

After we eat, I dish out some ice cream and Peanut looks at the little bowl with such awe it makes me wonder what in the world her life was like before whatever set her out in the brush where she was almost killed by fire. Nothing made a lot of sense to me, and later, while she sits on the floor wearing the new pajamas I bought for her, I look at Gwen, hoping she'll understand all my questions and worries. Gwen looks at me and then slips her hand in mine. It doesn't do a damned thing to answer any of the questions but it does a whole hell of a lot to ease the worry.

Later, we tuck Peanut in and while we sit waiting for her to fall asleep, she leaps up and throws her arms around Gwen. That's new for her and I can tell it touches

Gwen a great deal. She kisses Peanut's cheek and tucks her back in. When we leave five or ten minutes later, Peanut is sleeping and there's almost a smile on her face. I lead Gwen to the kitchen and open the liquor cabinet.

"She's opening up," I say.

"Not really," Gwen says. "Not yet. What she's doing is feeling safe. She's feeling safe and it's a new experience for her. That tells me she doesn't feel safe in general, that safety hasn't ever been a part of her life."

"It's not just the trauma from the fire?"

She takes the glass I hand her and gingerly sips it. I didn't even look at what I poured. I look at the bottle and smile because it's a two-hundred-dollar bottle of bourbon I got as a Christmas gift from my grandfather almost fifteen years ago. All at once, I decide Gwen is worth it. Of course, I also decide I'm being idiotic for starting to think of Gwen as something permanent rather than temporary. I pour a few fingers for myself and sip it.

It's pretty damned good.

I realize she hasn't answered and I say, "It's not just the trauma from the fire?"

She says, "No, I heard you. I'm just thinking. I don't think she even considers the fire traumatic. I think she thinks of it as something wonderful, a sudden reversal of fortune that brought you into her life. I don't think the fire traumatizes her at all."

"My God," I say. I drain my drink and set the glass down." I don't have any idea how to..." I let the words trail off.

She reaches forward and puts her hand on my chest. "You showed up and rescued her. I think that's probably one of your best qualities."

I try to come up with an answer to that but I can't. She smiles and says, "The girl was already traumatized and you rescued her from more than the flames." Gwen slides her hand down and takes mine. She puts her drink down and leads me to the bedroom.

My mind is swirling with a million thoughts and emotions and I can't get them organized. It doesn't really matter, though, because we get to the bedroom and I just don't care much about trying to figure those things out at the moment.

CHAPTER SEVEN

Gwen

I'm alive.

That's really what all of this comes down to. I am alive again, and there is something about that fact that terrifies me. Of course, it also brings with it emotions I never expected to feel again, emotions such as hope, joy, excitement, and anticipation. I actually wake up in the morning and look forward to the day. The concept is so foreign to me. In fact, it takes me a moment to process it.

For what seems as long as I can remember, sex has been no more for me than morning masturbation in the showerhead. It's just physical release, a vain attempt to accept physical pleasure as a replacement for emotional pleasure. The times in the past I've picked up a man at a bar for a one-night stand (or sometimes for two or three nights spread out over a month) there is no emotion. Sure,

I fake emotion. Unlike in the shower, I moan and act passionately while it happens. I'm certainly not going to treat someone like they're just a dildo to me.

But there is never any emotion. It is perfunctory to me, a simple physical exercise with a climax as the goal and whatever tiny bit of satisfaction that climax can give me so I somehow can keep from just disappearing into nothingness, crushed by the weight of all I've heard and seen.

But not now!

After two weeks of whatever this relationship with Barrett should be called, I wake with excitement and look forward to what the day brings. I am no longer a robot but a person. It is beautiful and it is frightening. The beautiful part is obvious. The frightening part isn't difficult to figure out either. Robots have hard, protective metal shells. Humans are soft and vulnerable.

I roll onto my side and I see this man with the perfect body sleeping next to me. Barret has both arms up and behind him so his head rests on his hands. The blanket is down to just above his ribcage. The position of his arms makes his incredible chest appear even more broad and muscular. I follow the sight of his large, defined biceps. They are almost on display now just because his arms are bent. It is strange to study this man's body is something I can only describe as pleased fascination.

I can't wait any longer.

I lean forward and kiss his throat, sliding on top of him and then down, kissing his breastbone and then his abdomen as I make my way to my destination. He wakes when I'm at his navel and he gently moves the blanket to the side. I look up at his face as I kiss below his navel and then lower. His eyes study me with what I imagine is the same fascination. They close halfway and he draws in a breath when my mouth reaches his cock and my kisses make their way down his shaft to the head. He draws in breath again as I use my tongue to scoop the head up and into my mouth.

I feel a thrill and go about the blowjob with a great deal of energy and enthusiasm. I don't know why I'm so desperate to please him. No, it isn't that I am desperate to please him, actually. I'm just desperate for him to experience pleasure. There's a difference. What matters to me is how much he enjoys it and not at all how it reflects on me. He reaches for me and I have a split second of conflict in my mind. I want to finish him with my mouth but I also want to feel him inside of me. In the end, it is my hesitation when it comes to making a decision that decides it. I'm up and looking at his face before I've settled on an answer. He rolls over and I'm beneath him after that. There's simply no way in hell I'll be changing a damned thing once his cock slips into me.

We make love in a way that contrasts pretty significantly with my aggressive attempt at a blowjob. I feel his weight above me and that's about the only thing that's even mildly imposing about the circumstances. He moves gently and sensually and somehow, it sends me to an incredible place that's not just physical but wrapped up in all of my newfound emotions, emotions I can finally embrace. When my orgasm hits, I am swept away by it and don't explode into movement like I ordinarily might. When he finishes, I feel a similar sweeping away. He remains still above me for a minute or two and then kisses me. I whisper, "Wow."

He kisses me again and says, "You said it." He pulls on his pajama bottoms and then goes to check on Peanut while I shower. A minute later, I hear him say, "You got a delivery. Two boxes."

"From my office," I say. "My regular work files and also files on all the currently missing girls under the age of fourteen. You can get started if you want. You know, just set aside kids ten or older or kids who don't match her skin or whatever. I can do it when I get out, too, though."

"I feel like we're getting somewhere," he says. "I'll get started."

I smile as he walks away and thinks about how different it is to take a shower and not to do it like it's some routine maintenance or something. I really believe this man, this magic firefighter, has changed me and rescued me. I feel like I'm okay now. I'm a real person again who hasn't forced all feelings away. I get out of the shower and dry off happily. Then, I walk out and see him in the living room. There are files spread out on the floor. He looks up at me and his face is... God, it's ashen, white.

"What's wrong?" I ask.

He looks at me and says, "How? How do you?" He stands up and shakes his head. "How can you even stand?

How do you not just shrink up into a ball and stay in bed all day? How can you... I see tears in his eyes as he says, "I think you must be the strongest person on Earth."

"I don't..." I look at the floor. The files aren't the missing person's files. Of course, he wouldn't know which ones were which. Instead, he sees my case files, all I've dealt with. He sees what made me shrink into a shadow of a person.

He puts his arms around me and pulls me tightly to him and suddenly I'm weeping. I'm weeping for Celie Sanders, whose father burned her hand on the stove because she was sick and couldn't stop crying. She was five. She had appendicitis and, oddly, would have died if not for the burn, which got her to the hospital. I'm weeping for Elizabeth Valdez, who'd uncle became so enthusiastic while raping her that he broke her arm. She was seven. I'm weeping for Tomas Dain, who watched his mother and father killed for a gambling debt. I'm weeping for them and dozens of others.

"You never have to be strong for me," Barrett whispers. "And my arms are always open."

I cry for almost an hour. Then, my phone alarm rings. It's seven o'clock. If I were still at the office, this alarm would remind me to show up early to prepare for my weekly meeting with Allen, my boss.

Right now, it reminds me that Peanut will wake at any moment. I back away and kiss Barrett briefly. "Right now," I say, "You're how I keep from curling up in a ball."

I kiss him again and say, "I better go splash some water on my face before Peanut wakes up."

As I walk into the bedroom to do just that it occurs to me that it's only now, after crying while Barrett held me, that I can really call myself okay.

And I am. I'm okay.

CHAPTER EIGHT

Barrett

I don't have any frame of reference for this. Sometimes, it feels like Peanut is right on the verge of telling us something important but then abruptly clams up again. Whoever frightened this little girl did it in a particularly powerful way. Her accent is impossible to trace. She's just an American child, five or six years old. She might come from anywhere in seventy-five percent of the country. In fact, only heavy accents like the deep, deep south, and thick New York or New Jersey can be absolutely ruled out. She doesn't use any obvious idioms.

We know nothing about her and Gwen says we can't press her. She says pressing her might make her withdraw completely and if she does, we'll never get her to come out of her shell. The whole situation is damned hard to accept but what the hell is the alternative to waiting? We just have to continue to build trust with Peanut and hope at some point she'll be willing to talk to us so we can come up with something that will give us an understanding of what there is in this girl's past that troubles her so much.

There's nothing else at all for us to do for her, nothing at all.

Damn it all to hell!

All of these thoughts come to me as I move through the forests. I come across a deer, and I'm so damned angry I almost kill the damned thing just because I'm pissed off. I'm not hungry, though, and I hold back on my more animal desires. Killing a deer might give brief satisfaction but that burst of energy won't actually solve a damned thing, just as trying to force the situation with Peanut won't force a damned thing either.

At least now Peanut trusts Gwen. She trusts Gwen enough that I am out here. I can't stay as long as I want because Gwen guesses two and a half hours is Peanut's limit. A half-hour drive here and a half hour back means I get a total of an hour and a half and I'm closing in on that. I talked to her three times on the phone in the half-hour drive out and the moment I shift back and get ready to leave, I will call her again.

I make my way through the forest and back to the car but I don't bask in the sun. I can easily lose track of time when I do that and I'm not sure I want to risk it. Instead, I shift back, get in the car and dial home. Gwen answers and there's no stress or worry in her voice, which tells me things went well. "Would you like to talk to Barrett Peanut?" she asks as she puts me on speaker.

"Yes, please," Peanut says. She asks, "Are you coming back?"

"I am," I reply. "I'll be there in about thirty minutes." I realize every phone conversation starts with her asking if I am coming back. "What do you say when I get there, we do something fun?"

"Can you give me a ride?"

That's intriguing. "Where to?"

"Wherever dragons go," she says.

I smile and say, "Well, I'll have to figure out a good place where dragons go that's also good for little girls. How about instead of that, I ask Gwen if she'll drive you to a very special restaurant with Pizza and games and I'll meet you two there?"

"Really? I can go there? You'll take me? I don't have to stay inside?" She fires the questions off so quickly and they're all filled with the same sense of wonder she showed the time I gave her a little bowl of ice cream for the first time.

"Yes, yes, yes, yes," I say. "We're going to have a lot of fun. Sound good?"

"Sounds good!" she says. I love hearing the excitement in her voice.

"Okay. Give the phone to Gwen for me, okay?"

"Ohhhhhh Kay!" she says. I recall her watching a show with a lead character who says that just this morning. I laugh and there appears to be laughter in Gwen's voice when she answers.

"It appears you 've made a certain little girl very happy," Gwen says.

In the background, I hear Peanut say, "She means me! I the girl but I'm not a curtain!"

I chuckle at that as well, share my plan for the combination pizza joint and game room and think about just how happy I am at the moment. The feeling remains for the rest of the day and when I tuck Peanut in at the end of the night, I realize all of my high horse crap about shifters and pure humans not mixing is pretty much bullshit.

I pull the blankets up to her chin. She clings to the enormous stuffed bunny I won for her at a carnival game at the pizza place. She's already asleep, exhausted from all the activity. I lean forward and give her a kiss on her forehead. She seems to smile in her sleep but, of course, the way I'm feeling it's highly possible the smile is just my imagination.

I walk out of the room and see Gwen on the couch smiling at me. She has a big stuffed animal, too, this one is a very goofy-looking blue flamingo. I walk over and sit down next to her. "I have a confession to make," I say. "I'm really a..." I pause realizing I intend to tell her about my serpent instead of my feelings about her and more presently, Peanut.

"Are you making a joke?" she asks with another smile.

"No," I say. "No, that's not..." I take a breath. "I'm really an asshole. I tucked Peanut in and all I could think about was how I don't want to lose her. All I could think about was how if we never find out who she is that won't happen." I sigh and say, "and there will never be a reason for you to leave."

Her mouth parts and she draws in breath sharply. I don't know if the response indicates a positive emotion or a negative one. She finally says, "Finding out the truth about Peanut isn't going to give me a reason to leave."

I don't know if there is more she wants to say on the subject. If there is, she doesn't get a chance because my mouth finds hers and as I hold her, I feel like the chances of me letting go anytime soon are very, very low.

CHAPTER NINE

Gwen

I lay in bed next to Barrett, breathing heavily after a particularly breathtaking bout of sex. I just don't understand how this sexy fireman can be gently romantic and sensual one time and extraordinarily intense the next time. I have no complaints, of course. On the contrary, I think I'm about as happy about that as I can be.

Happy.

God, what a weird thing to feel after so long not being able to even conceive of happiness as something possible for me. That's how I feel when I'm with Barrett, though. I feel that way with Peanut, too. Something still frightens her but she's not damaged. She's going to be fine. I can see the resilience in her eyes. She's a strong little girl.

I can also tell that a great deal of her strength comes

from her trusting Barrett. It isn't strange that a child might trust the man who saved her life. In fact, depending on how powerfully traumatic the experience was for her, she may think of Barrett as unimpeachably good. I smile at the thought. I certainly think of Barrett as unimpeachably good in some ways.

I guess I actually feel like he's unimpeachably good in a number of ways. We've only been together for days, can't even measure it in weeks, really, I think. That's way too early for me to be filled with the kinds of thoughts I have about him. Too early or not, they're here and I'm filled with them. It seems so strange to me to feel this way, particularly because I fought for so long to make emotion something I just didn't experience.

I can't resist him enough not to risk everything. Although I spend a great deal of time worrying about the possibility of slipping back into the emptiness, at the moment the only thing that matters to me is right now.

And right now, is Barrett next to me.

I slide down under the blankets and then carefully slip over him between his legs. I don't know how long he'll sleep and I want him to wake with my mouth surrounding his shaft for I don't hesitate. I just close my lips over his soft cock and suck him all the way in. I pulse my mouth and move my tongue and if there is anything more exhila-rating than the feel of his cock stiffening in my mouth, I have yet to experience it. I love the way his body reacts and I keep my lips right down at the base and suck firmly as he grows hard.

I finally have to back up a little but I keep moving my tongue as I suck my way to the tip. Then, I plunge down again, hold myself there so he's fully in my mouth and throat, and then suck slowly back up. I do that two more times and then I feel the blankets come off. The knowledge he's awake thrills me and makes my pussy seem to pulse with need. What a dramatic change from the perfunctory masturbation and emotionless, stress-release one-night stands in my recent past!

If there's one thing I really love about Barrett, and God, there have to be about a million things I love about him, it's that he's never completely predictable with me. I think I'm giving a damned good blowjob, and I always feel powerful about blowjobs when I give them to him because it makes me feel almost like I'm in complete control with this giant of a man despite the pretty damned dramatic difference in our size. But he lifts me suddenly and his cock is out of my mouth. I prepare to feel him thrust up into me but he changes the position and suddenly, I'm on all fours. I gasp as his cock slides into me from this position.

I scream into the blankets, pressing my face as hard as I can into the bedclothes so the scream will be muffled and Peanut won't hear us. God, it's amazing to have to worry about hiding my reactions. It adds an element of naughtiness to the situation that drives me wild with need. It makes me feel almost impossibly good. It reminds me of my younger days of first experimentation with sex when getting caught was the biggest worry. Barrett holds tightly to my waist as he thrusts into me and I feel my body get right to the edge of orgasm in almost no time at all.

It's almost like Barrett has the ability to increase my capacity for pleasure to something well beyond what any girl has the right to expect. That in and of itself is amazing but the really remarkable thing is he not only increases my capacity for pleasure but also somehow drives that pleasure so the increased capacity is very quickly used up.

And then I get more than I can handle!

His thrusts feel exquisite one moment, overpowering the next, impossible to take a moment later, and then so need-inducing that I beg for more. Thankfully, my body is pushed to the limit so my begging ends up whispers instead of shouts. "God! Yes, Barrett. Oh God, please. Yes! Yes!" I don't think Barrett actually needs any encouragement from me as he thrusts into me, and as my orgasm hits, my ability to speak disappears. I kind of just stop everything I'm doing and remain in the position as though I'm locked with my shoulders on the bed, my face pressed against the blanket, and my ass in the air. Barrett doesn't stop. He moves his body like a jackhammer and keeps thrusting into me until I think I could just cease to exist and become nothing more than the memory of sensation.

I still exist four or five minutes later when he's spent and he gently withdraws from me, leans down and kisses my ear, and then says, "Good morning, Baby."

I feel a warm kind of excitement and giggle. It's not

the sex that does it. It's his term of endearment. I realize I love this man. I'm in love, and it's pretty damned shocking because I didn't think I could ever love anyone. Hell, I'm only now discovering that I can feel again. Throughout the day, the feeling of joy and love grows and there must be something in my expression that makes it obvious because Peanut is particularly giggly and stays close to me the whole day.

I'm particularly surprised to realize I not only love Barrett but I love Peanut, too. That's an unwise thing in my profession but I'm learning I can't help what I can't help. Not long ago, my way of dealing with that reality, that I'm helpless to change certain things, almost destroyed me. It will never happen again. It will hurt when we get Peanut back where she belongs but I can't help but love her now. As for Barrett and me, I can only hold fast to the hope that how I feel about him is more than how we both feel about this little girl.

I need to tell him I love him.

He falls down onto the bed next to me and says, "Sometimes I wonder how I survive sex with you." I giggle at that and snuggle close. "And I also wonder how I could ever survive without you." I lift up my head and he says, "Not just for the sex. I mean, don't stop the sex." I giggle again and he puts his hand on my cheek. "Gwendolyn Anjanette Montgomery, I love you."

I stare at him for a second, shocked into speechlessness. For Christ's sake, I was just deciding to tell him that same thing! I finally manage to blurt out, "Barrett I forgot your last name, I love you, too."

He pulls me close and if there is a world record for the most perfect kiss, we break it.

CHAPTER TEN

Barrett

Peanut smiles a hell of a lot more now.

So, she's a lot like me and, as near as I can tell, a lot like Gwen.

We sit at the little breakfast table in the kitchen putting together pigs in a blanket, and little cocktail sausages wrapped in biscuit dough. She loves doing it and especially loves when I give her a fork and tell her she can make designs on the dough part.

She's a different girl altogether.

Sometimes I forget there's a mystery to solve about her.

When they're all ready to go, I walk with her to the preheated oven. I let her open the oven door but I put the tray in myself. I close the door and turn on the light. "We can check on it in eight minutes to see how they're doing," I say.

"Can I watch before then?" she asks. "Can I stay here and watch?"

My first inclination is to tell her she is certain to be bored out of her skull. Instead, I get a chair and put it in front of the stove. "Don't touch the door of the oven in case it gets hot, okay?"

"Okay, Barrett," she says.

Gwen steps into the kitchen, fresh from the shower and hair still wet. She walks up and looks to make sure Peanut isn't looking. Then, she quickly and quietly kisses me. Peanut immediately says, "I like when you kiss."

Gwen looks horrified for a moment but as I chuckle, she smiles. "Why do you like that?" she asks.

"Because," Peanut says, "people who kiss each other a lot are nice."

"Do you know a lot of people who kiss each other a lot?" Gwen asks.

"No," Peanut says, "only two people."

I see the confusion and the concern on Gwen's face and she finally asks, "Do you know a lot of people who aren't nice?"

"Only two," the little girl says and she doesn't elaborate.

Gwen looks at me and tries a different tack. "What are you cooking, Peanut?"

"Sausage horns," she replies.

"Sausage horns?" Both Gwen and I ask at the same time.

"But I like the way Barrett cooks them better."

"Better than what?" I ask.

"Then the other way."

I'm about to ask but Gwen lifts her hand. "Barrett and I are going to go to the backyard to check on the flowers. Will you be okay here?"

"Yes," she says, "except I don't know when the sausage horns will be done."

"We'll be back before they're ready," I say, "but if they suddenly turn orange and purple you have to run and get me, okay?"

She giggles and says, "That's silly."

"Well silly can be fun," I reply.

I follow Gwen to the sliding glass door and we step outside. "That was from her past," she says.

"Yeah. I called them pigs in a blanket."

She nods. "But it means she's starting to include her past in conversations without thinking about it at all."

"That's good, right?"

Gwen says, "I think so. I mean, this is a pretty innocent kind of thing but it came out naturally. We want more of those things to happen."

"But how do I know what to talk to her about?"

Gwen shrugs. "You don't. There's no way to figure it out. You just have to keep doing things with her and let her make associations and share them."

"All right," I say. "Should we go inside and start?"

"Sure," she replies, "we can see what happens when you get the food out of the oven."

"Oh," I say, "I thought we were going in there to kiss a lot in front of her."

She rolls her eyes with a laugh and punches my shoulder. "Hey now!" I say, "You don't want to frighten the kid!"

She rolls her eyes again and turns around. When she gets to the door, she wiggles her ass suggestively just to screw with me and I lunge for her but can't land the swat before she's inside and says, "We're back! How are the sausage horns doing?"

The food is fine and breakfast is fine. After, Gwen kisses me goodbye, and Peanut giggles. Gwen kisses Peanut goodbye and I try to impersonate the giggles. That sends the little girl into a laughing fit that might be the purest expression of joy I've ever heard or seen in my life. Gwen leaves to check in with her office and I lift Peanut up and tickle her for a minute or two before I get her onto the couch and set her up with coloring books and crayons.

As she colors, I break out my laptop. I'm not all that Internet Savvy so I end up making several calls to the station house. There are a few guys there who probably could have become software developers if they didn't get into firefighting and there's another guy there who majored in marketing and by the time he graduated college had an online marketing firm worth a few million dollars. He became a firefighter when a friend of his died in a fire shortly after graduation.

With them helping me and plenty of coloring books, toys, and videos to keep Peanut occupied, I'm able to do a whole lot of research. I make Peanut a grilled cheese sandwich and cut it into strips. She laughs as I set out bowls of lava for her to dip them in. She gets more ketchup on her face than in her mouth. After I get her cleaned up, I set her down for a nap and she fall asleep almost instantly. I get back to my research on the internet.

And I can't believe it but I figure it all out.

No. That's premature.

A better way to put it is that I think I have it all figured out. It's horrifying, actually, if my guess is right. I think about what that little girl has been through and I think about the circumstances that miraculously brought her into my life. If what I've discovered is accurate, we finally have answers and Peanut might finally have a chance to overcome the challenges behind her.

I can't be completely sure, though. All I have is online news articles and those articles don't offer me a great deal of information. The information they do offer is really just a starting point. I don't have the resources or the necessary database to test my theory. I don't have what it takes to figure out the full picture.

But I know a sexy and beautiful child psychologist who does.

I pick up the phone and dial Gwen.

CHAPTER ELEVEN

Gwen

Things are strange. As I walk into the office, I realize I'm actually happy to be here. I haven't felt that way in as long as I can remember. For so long, the obligation is the only thing that keeps me going. Although I can't help the children I must analyze and interview, the role I play nonetheless does some good so even though it makes me terribly empty inside and forces me to drive my emotions out of me with all the power I can muster. Obligation has kept me going for so long!

And now, there is more.

It is almost like Barrett give me permission to feel again. In addition, I know that we are helping Peanut even if there is no way to get to a point of diagnosis yet. I don't know what it is I can do for her yet but I know that she is losing a great deal of her fear. She is having full conversations, as long as those conversations don't press her about her life before her rescue from the fire. We're making a difference, though, and that's powerful.

I sit behind my desk and realize there aren't any issues to deal with. I have two depositions I will need to get to as soon as possible. These are depositions for upcoming trials. I make some calls to the DA and get them scheduled, one for this afternoon and one for tomorrow. Other than that, I have two reports to review and submit. Everything else is just continuing the work with Peanut. I send a quick update to my boss about her but he steps into my office just as I hit send.

"Anything yet?" he asks.

"She's going to be fine, Allen," I say, "which is a relief, of course. She's still not ready to talk. We still don't have her actual name. She's fine, though, for now."

"Why for now?" Allen asks.

"Because at some point, when we figure out who she is, she'll have to leave Barrett and she's so attached to him she might actually think of him as the embodiment of safety."

"I've been in touch with the fire chief," Allen says, "and he tells me Barrett is free to take as long as he needs to see this through. He has some great things to say about him, too."

"That's a relief," I say. I mean, of course, that Barrett is free to do the work with Peanut but I also feel oddly proud that his boss likes him.

"As for you," Allen says, "I can keep you on a half

schedule for the immediate future. Ultimately, give me a shift or two a week here at the office but you're on call the rest of the time in case you're needed."

"Thanks, Allen," I reply.

He looks at me and then closes the door, walks up, and sits down across from me. "You're alive again, Sweetheart."

I smile. "Oh, Uncle Allen! I... Well, it's just that I..."

He laughs. "You and this firefighter, huh?"

I blush like crazy but nod. He says, "When you moved in with your aunt and me, we wanted to make sure you grew up in a way that would make your parents proud. You're that girl, Gwenny. I know my brother is looking down from Heaven very proud of you." I blush a little at his praise. He smiles and says, "and I'm glad I don't have to fire you."

"Fire me?"

He shrugs. "You were killing yourself, retreating into a shell. I planned on firing you. Aunt Helen and I already had money set aside to set you up in private practice. I couldn't let you go on doing this."

"When?"

He smiles. "You would already be gone if not for that little girl."

I look at him for a while and then laugh. "I don't know if I should yell at you or thank you?"

He assumes a very sad expression and says, "You're welcome." Then he smiles brightly and says, "There you go. I covered all the bases with the response."

I giggle and say, "I love you, Uncle Allen. I'm wrapped up here for today and I'm going to get back to B... to that little girl. We call her Peanut."

He raises an eyebrow. "Nice try. Go ahead and get back to your fireman."

"The little girl, too!" I say and he laughs and lifts his hands up in surrender. I leave the office feeling pretty damned good about things.

And I head right back in before I even get to my car. My uncle sees me and says, "What's up?"

"Barrett figured it out!" I say.

"Figured what out?"

"Susana Pedersen," I say, "with a *d*. That's the little girl."

"How the hell did he do that?"

I laugh. "Google."

"What?" he asks as I head into my office and sit down.

"She called pigs in a blanket by another name, and he went online and found out that the Danish word for them is *sausage horns*." I tap my keyboard and he sits down across from me.

"You're not making a damned bit of sense," Allen says.

"He made them with her for breakfast this morning, you know with the refrigerated dough for croissants and little breakfast sausages. After they went in the oven, she called them sausage horns instead of pigs in a blanket, which is how he described them. So, he went online and figured out the word for them in Danish is..." by now I've got a site in front of me "... *Pølsehorn*, which translates directly as sausage horns."

"My God," he says, "it was that simple?"

"That simple? You know how many sausage-making equipment results he had to look through before he could figure that out?" I laugh and Uncle Allen points at me.

"You've fallen hard for this guy."

I push that to the side and say, "Anyway, he used the Denmark connection to find a missing little girl. A year and a half ago. The mother committed..." My voice changes because it doesn't feel all that exciting to me anymore. "The mother committed suicide and they couldn't find the little girl. The investigators believe a couple named Mark and Christy Wolnak have her. They think the mother, planning suicide, gave them to the couple."

"Why not give her to the state?"

"The mother's parents, who emigrated from Denmark, died when she was six. She spent her whole life in the system."

"And she didn't want her daughter to do that. She must have trusted the couple."

I nod. "Anyway, all of that was just newspaper articles from a year and a half ago. The couple disappeared. So that's all he could figure out."

"Because he can't do what we can do."

I nod and get to work.

I spend a lot of time crying over the next few hours and I'm damned lucky my uncle is there to keep me on track. Peanut has been through hell. Mark and Christy Wolnak are assumed names. Child abusers often create fake names when they are released from prison.

I finally get all the information together I need and pack it into a folder. I break down again and I don't really know how long I cry but I lift my head when I hear a clink. Uncle Alex smiles softly. On my desk is a glass tumbler filled with amber liquid. "You need it," he says.

I take a swallow and it burns like hell going down but he's right. I lift the glass to my lips again as warmth settles over me. He sits down and we talk about all the implications and the next steps. It takes about an hour but he makes me wait another hour before he lets me drive home to Barrett and Peanut.

CHAPTER TWELVE

Barrett

"Peanut," Gwen calls, "Could you please come over here?" Peanut gets up off the couch and walks toward where Gwen sits at the table. There is a chair pulled out a bit for her and she sits down and waits placidly. "I want to tell you something but I'm a little bit worried you might become upset when I tell you. Do you know why I'm worried?"

Peanut shakes her head. Gwen says, "I'm worried because I like you. I like you and I don't want you to feel upset. I don't want you to be sad or scared. Do you understand?"

"You don't want my heart to hurt," she says.

I set a cup of juice and some sliced apples on a plate in front of the little girl and then sit down next to her. "That's a very good way to put it," I say, "so will you do your best not to be upset when Gwen tells you what she wants to tell you?"

Peanut nods solemnly and says, "I don't want your heart to hurt. I don't want Gwen's heart to hurt either."

Gwen extends her hand, sliding it across the table. I'm happy to see Peanut put her hand on top of Gwen's. "Peanut," Gwen says, "I think the name you're not allowed to say is Susana." The girl's eyes grow wide and Gwen says, "Is that right."

Peanut looks at me, clearly frightened. I nod and say, "It's okay. You can tell us."

She turns and looks at Gwen. She says in a very quiet voice, "Yes."

"I don't want your heart to hurt, Peanut, but I need to tell you what I think happened and I need you to tell me if I'm right. Can you try to do that for me?"

Peanut says, "Okay." Her voice sounds like she's decidedly not okay.

Gwen says, "I think you used to have a mommy and she was sad a lot. I think she tried to be happy but she couldn't. One day, she thought that she was being a bad mommy because she was always sad and she thought you should have a happy mommy. Even though she knew that it would make her even sadder, she decided to give you to a new Daddy and Mommy so you wouldn't have her as a sad mommy."

Peanut stares at her and I can see her bottom lip quivering. I reach for her and lift her up, holding her to me. She puts her head on my shoulder and turns it so she's looking at Gwen. "Is that what happened?" Gwen asks. I feel Peanut nodding. I look over her head and I'm pleased to see Peanut is still holding her hand. Gwen says, "but your mommy didn't know the new daddy and mommy were very bad people, did she?"

"No," Peanut whispers. "I was too much work for Mommy."

"Did your mommy tell you that?" I feel her shake her head. Gwen asks, "Was it the new mommy and daddy who told you that?" I feel her head move again. I can't tell if she's shaking or nodding. Gwen says, "Well they lied to you. Your mommy was trying to give you a good life but she didn't know how to. She was sad. She didn't know that you wanted to be with her even if she was sad." I feel Susana nodding and Gwen adds, "And there are some things much worse than having a sad mommy, aren't there?"

Peanut nods again but says nothing. Gwen says, "Peanut, I need to do something really scary now. Before I do, I want you to know that you will never, ever, ever go back to the bad daddy and mommy, okay?"

"Are you sure?" Peanut asks.

"It will never happen."

"Because of Barrett?" I have no idea where that came from.

"Because of another reason," Gwen says. "But I need to show you some pictures and I need you to tell me if you see someone in the pictures. I need you to tell me if you see the bad mommy and daddy, okay?"

"And you won't let them get me?"

"I won't," Gwen says.

Peanut looks at me and says, "And you'll turn into a dragon and eat them if they try?"

My God. She saw my snake when I rescued her. I look at Gwen, who is understandably confused. I look back at Peanut and say, "If anyone ever tries to hurt you, I'll turn into a dragon and stop them."

She looks at me and nods solemnly. She turns to Gwen and says, "Okay. I'll look. I won't be scared."

Gwen looks at me and then at Peanut. She sighs and says, "Okay." She takes out several mugshots of women. She puts them down and says, "Is one of these the bad mommy?" Peanut is on the brink of tears as she leans over and points to one.

"Good girl," I say. "You're really helping, honey."

Gwen gathers up the photos and does the same with the men. This time, Peanut does cry as she points one out. I hold her as she weeps and Gwen gathers up the pictures. She reaches forward and strokes Peanut's hair. "Sweetheart," she says, "You'll never see them again. They're gone forever."

Peanut stops crying and lifts herself up to look at Gwen. "I think I know what happened, Peanut. I think the bad daddy and mommy were fighting. I think they did that a lot. I think they were fighting and you didn't like that because whenever they fought the bad daddy would come and hurt you. You were in a motor home, right? A house that's also a car?"

Peanut nods her head.

"And you did something very brave. While they were fighting by the campfire, you ran away and you kept running." Again, Peanut nods. "And you ran for a long time and you didn't know where you were going but then there was a big fire and that's when Barrett saved you."

Peanut nods again. I lift her chin and kiss her forehead. "That was very brave to run away from the bad people."

"And you turned into a dragon to save me," she says.

Gwen frowns and then says, "Peanut, the bad mommy and the bad daddy won't ever bother you again. The bad mommy killed the bad daddy and when the police tried to arrest her, she tried to kill them. The police killed her instead. You'll never have to worry about them taking you ever again."

Peanut looks at Gwen and it's impossible to see if she can actually comprehend what's being said. Finally, she says, "Never ever?"

"Never ever," Gwen says.

Peanut looks at me and says, "And if a different bad mommy and daddy try to take me, you won't let them, right?"

"That's right," I say.

"Because you'll change into a dragon, right?"

I glance at Gwen and then back at peanut. "That's right," I say. I glance at Gwen again. She's unreadable.

I order Chinese food and make Peanut laugh by pretending the egg rolls are little people. At the end of the night, we get her tucked in and head out to the kitchen. Gwen says, "I can arrange temporary custody," she says.

"You mean, she can stay?"

She nods. "You'll be her custodian."

"What does temporary mean?"

"It's a legal term more than anything else," Gwen says. "Essentially, you'll be a foster parent without being a foster parent. The state won't pay you and they won't breathe down your neck either."

"You can make that happen?"

"If you want."

"Hell yes, I want!" I realize I'm shouting and I lift up my hands. "Sorry. Will you…" I take a deep breath. "Will you stay, too?"

Gwen nods and smiles. "I seem to recall something about loving you. I seem to recall something about you loving me."

I lean forward and kiss her tenderly but then back up. "Then we probably ought to talk about the dragon thing."

She nods. "I don't think it's a problem to let her have that fantasy right now but we'll need to ease her out of it."

I take a deep breath. This is either going to be a perfect night or a terrible night. "It's not a fantasy," I say. I take another breath, "and it's not a dragon."

CHAPTER THIRTEEN

Gwen

The four weeks that pass after telling Peanut about the fate of her abusers are a whirlwind. There are a lot of hoops to jump through but the upshot of being a child psychologist is that the hoops are really just paperwork for me. Uncle Allen helps as well, and custody of Peanut is settled in very short order.

As for the fact that I'm in love with a shifter?

I don't know if I just bury that truth or if I just refuse to think of Barrett as anything other than Barrett. Who knows? We're still together, though. In fact, my bed at my apartment remains made. I haven't slept there since the first night at Barrett's place.

And Peanut is blooming.

She's still not completely opened up and I realize when she engages in good behavior it's out of fear. She can't wrap it around her mind that her mother didn't get rid of her, that the woman was very sad and thought she was doing right by her daughter. I'm hoping I'll be able to explain it to her better when she's older.

Barrett pulls the car over and gets out. He opens the door for Peanut first and she hops out excitedly, bouncing and laughing and acting about as hyper as a kid can act. She looks so happy. It seems every day she gets just a little happier.

"Are you sure you're ready for this?" Barrett asks as he opens the door for me.

"It's okay," Peanut says. Her voice isn't soft or monotone. It's bright and even enthusiastic. "He's a very nice dragon."

"You're the first shifter I've ever known," I say, "I mean personally, anyway."

He smiles and says, "No. I'm just the first you know personally who also told you he was a shifter."

I put my hands on my hips and say, "told me? I think that's a pretty generous way to put it."

He flashes me a cocky smile and says, "I couldn't let you believe it was all in Peanut's imagination." It is impossible not to smile back at him.

I look at Peanut and say, "Are you sure this is what you want?"

Peanut nods firmly. "It's my birthday and this is my present!"

Barrett laughs and smiles at me. I think about the dining room table back home—God, I think of Barrett's house as home now. I think about all the presents and the cake I set up while he was buckling Peanut into her seat. "Can't disappoint the birthday girl, I guess," he says.

"Okay," I say with a smile. "Do I need to pick her up and turn her around? I mean, when you take your clothes off?"

"See that," he says. "You know something about shifters after all." I reach for Peanut and he says, "but no. That's just for the boring warm-blooded shifters, not for the super cool and exciting shifters like me."

Peanut giggles and I roll my eyes. "All right, Mr. Cool and Exciting," I say. He nods and shifts.

There is nothing to prepare me for it.

Oh, sure, he's described his serpent, which is essentially a giant diamondback rattlesnake except he doesn't have the markings and he's green instead of sand colored. So, he looks like a viper but he's green, deep green. I can understand why Peanut thinks he's a dragon.

He's huge.

He's fucking terrifying.

A million things run through my head and chief among them is the realization I can't do this. There's no way I can be with Barrett no matter how much I love him. How can I possibly find any common ground with a creature so vastly different, so dangerous? How can—

I gasp and cry out, "Peanut!"

It's too late. She runs forward and puts her hands on his massive body. The head comes down and she hugs it. "See? See? He's a nice dragon. He's a very nice dragon."

His head comes down so it's flat on the ground and Peanut giggles as she just climbs on top of the giant thing. She giggles again as it lifts up and suddenly, she's climbing onto the massive back.

She's laughing and I say, "Are you sure that's a good idea?"

She's completely giggly. She looks at me and says, "Come on! Come on! We're going for a ride! Come on, Mommy!"

I stare at her in shock.

Suddenly, Barrett's serpent is far less important than what I just heard that little girl say. I wonder for a moment if I just misheard her but as I step a little closer, she says brightly, "See? He's not scary. Come on up."

I overcome my fear and step up. I look down and say, "I hope you can carry me."

The big snake head lifts up and I stare in wonder as it moves up and down in a nod that reminds me of a cartoon snake in the movie about Robin Hood except with animals instead of people. His head comes down to the ground. "Go ahead," Peanut says. It's an entirely different world for me now, and I guess the truth is that Peanut is absolutely right. What I need to do is hop on and enjoy the ride.

So that's exactly what I do.

There's no real way to describe the size of him. I guess if King Kong was real, I would feel like Fay Wray. Peanut is in front of me and she leans back against me. Surprisingly, Barrett's serpent is a perfect size. It's a lot like being on horseback, I guess. My feet are about four and a half feet up off the ground. My legs are spread but not uncomfortably.

"Okay, Peanut," I say, "are you ready?"

She giggles and says, "Ready, Betty!" I have no idea where she got that from but it's cute and wonderful to hear.

"Okay," I say. "You can go ahead, Barrett."

There's no way to describe what it's like when he starts moving. I'm terrified for about two minutes even as Peanut cackles with glee. I get into the spirit of things soon, though, and most of the half-hour ride is nothing short of absolutely exhilarating. By the time he stops and his head comes up so I can deposit Peanut on top and he can set her down, I feel wonderful.

And any worry or fear about the situation is gone.

I swing myself over and slide to the ground, feeling kind of cool about being able to do that. Peanut smiles at me but I don't think she's smiling about how I got off Barrett's viper. I think she's just attuned to our emotions and senses our happiness. Abused children often become very adept at reading adults. They have to.

I stare at the giant snake and I'm about to reach for it but suddenly it's gone and Barrett is standing there again. Peanut says, "Yay!"

Barrett looks at me and I stare at him in wonder. "I don't know what to say," I finally get out, "It's...it's breathtaking.'"

"Breathtaking good or bad?"

"Good, silly!" Peanut says.

I laugh and say, "Yeah. Good, silly."

Barret smiles and says, "Are you ready, little girl?"

"Ready, Freddy!" she says.

I chuckle. "How many more of those does she have?"

Barrett says, "about a million. Okay. Go ahead, Peanut."

Peanut nods importantly and takes my hand. She pulls me a foot or so away and then knees abruptly. "Will you marry Barrett?" she asks.

I stare at her in shock and then turn around in shock. It takes me a half second to look down and realize Barrett is kneeling, holding out a ring. "Well?" he asks, "Will you marry me?"

I look at him and scream, "Yes! Yes!" Then, I try to hug him but it's too late. Peanut tackles me from behind and we tumble to the ground as she giggles and shouts triumphantly.

EPILOGUE

Gwen

I start my day like I always do. I don't get upset when my alarm rings. I just roll to the left and slide under the blankets to wake Barrett up with my mouth. There's a fifty/fifty chance on any given day that he won't let me finish and will screw me silly before he cums. If he doesn't and he finishes in my mouth, he's still just as likely to screw me like silly afterward. Today is a screw me like a silly day. After, I roll off the bed and head to the bathroom.

The breeze from the air conditioning vent passes over my naked body and sends goosebumps rising up all over me. I shiver and breathe out, "It's a chilly willy day!" I giggle and pad my way past my dresser and step into the bathroom. I walk directly to the shower and slide open the glass door so I can enter. I close it and turn the water on. The water is cold as it sprays over me. I shriek and back away until I can feel from the droplets that hit my feet that the water's warmed up. I test it just to be sure.

The water is warm and I wash my hair, smiling and sighing at the lovely scent of the floral shampoo. I hear the shower door open and say, "Come on in. The water's fine." A moment later, I feel the gently exfoliating washcloth on me as Barrett runs it over my body, filling the shower with the woodsy smell of the tea tree oil. I sigh again and let the water rinse me off. I grab the showerhead and then giggle when it doesn't move.

"What's so funny?" he asks.

"I forgot we're not at my condo," I say. "I wanted to use the shower hose to get you wet before I lather you up."

He smiles and puts his hands under my arms. He lifts me up and turns us around. "Brute!" I say. I punch his chest lightly as he leans back and the water courses over him. He doesn't have body wash. He uses a thick bar of pine tar soap, and so in just a few minutes, the scent of pine is added to the mix. I giggle and say, "We're going to end up with a whole forest in this shower."

"Absolutely fine by me," he says.

"Yeah, yeah, dragon boy."

"It's my snake, not my dragon," he says in mock surprise.

I reach forward and wrap my fingers around him. "There's only one snake of yours I'm interested in," I say.

"Dragon," he says quickly. "Yep. That's it indeed. My dragon."

I giggle and say, "You're just a pushover."

"I am not," he replies, "but beauty can always tame the beast."

A few minutes later, we're dried and dressed. When we step out of the room, I'm surprised to see Peanut standing up straight, already dressed and pretty close to dressed correctly. "Well look at that!" I say as I step up and kneel in front of her. I kiss her forehead and nonchalantly fix her buttons. Then, I tell her I need to make sure I put fresh socks in her sock drawer. I really just want to put her shoes on the right feet. They're Velcro-strap shoes so it doesn't take long to get them off. "Yep," I say. "Good socks." I stand up and say, "You got ready all by yourself! That's a pretty big girl thing to do."

She nods. "So you wouldn't have to worry about it."

Barrett crosses over to her and lifts her up into his arms. "Listen to me, Peanut," he says, "We're not going to change our mind. Never. Do you understand?"

"Even if I'm too much work?"

"You'll never be too much work," I say. "Never in a million years."

She looks at me and then at Barrett. Finally, she asks, "What about in a billion years?" in an exaggerated voice I know she got right out of a cartoon about a detective who's also a squirrel.

Barrett laughs and says, "Not in a billion plus a billion."

"Okay, Dragon Daddy," she says. She looks at me and says, "If you're already my Mommy and Barrett is already my Daddy, what does *getting adopted* mean?"

"Adopted means that the whole world knows that you're our daughter," Barrett says, "and it means you're going to have our last name so the whole world knows. It—"

"Like Mommy has your last name now?"

"Exactly like that," I say.

"And I'm going to be Susana Peterson," she says.

"Yup!"

"But you'll still call me Peanut."

"That's right," I say, "and it means that nobody can ever decide you shouldn't live with us. Nobody can ever take you away."

She smiles and says, "Does it mean I'll never be too much work?" Her question is sincere. It'll take time for her to feel completely secure.

"Didn't I just say not in a billion plus a billion?" Barrett asks.

Peanut nods and says, "Just checking."

"Okay," Barrett says, "What's our secret?"

"You got mommy a tennies bracelet for her birthday."

"A tennis bracelet!" I exclaim.

Barrett groans. "No. The other secret." He looks at me and I wiggle my eyebrows and tap my wrist.

"I don't tell anybody that you're really a dragon snake viper serpent." She says firmly.

"Good girl," he says and kisses her forehead.

"And I'll just pretend I didn't hear anything about any diamond bracelet I may or may not be getting." I chuckle. "Or a new pair of tennies."

He smiles and leans forward. "Good girl," he says and kisses my forehead. He turns to the little girl we will officially adopt in less than an hour and winks.

Peanut giggles and it sounds like music.

WHAT DID you think about Barrett and Gwen? If you're like me, you fell in love with Barrett right off the bat. He's sexy, strong, cocky, and... Well, if I keep going, I'll just daydream about him all day. I fell in love with Barrett when I wrote *Dangerous Serpent's Secret Desire* and I really fell in love with Gwen, too. Were you glad to see her let down her walls and embrace feelings again? Can you even imagine how hard it must have been for her? I'll tell you I really fell in love with Peanut and I'm glad she got the happy ending she deserves, too. I hope you liked this one, the eighth book in the *Company 417 Shifters* series. I loved writing about Barrett and Gwen and how they ended up with an instant family.

There are other firemen at Company 417!

In the next book of this incredible series, you're in for a great time. What do you get when you mix a large portion of suspense with a healthy helping of romance and add plenty of spicy sexiness to the recipe? You get our next hot story. Jeff O'Leary isn't the kind of guy to mess around. He's a no-nonsense kind of guy who doesn't have time for foolishness. When he wants something, he goes right after it whether it's a job, a meal, or a night with a beautiful girl. That focus is what allows him to save the life of Iris Fletcher when the office building where she works is engulfed in flames. She's captivating and everything he can imagine in a woman. He especially loves that she has the kind of personality that's strong and independent. She won't put up with anything! The fire wasn't an accident, though. Someone wants this fiery girl dead, and unless Jeff can figure out who and why the love he never thought he'd find will be taken from him. You don't want to miss this one. *Lusty Leopard's Fiery Girl is the next exciting shifter romance in the Company 417 Shifters series!*

ALSO BY AMELIA WILSON

www.ingramcontent.com/pod-product-compliance
Lightning Source LLC
Chambersburg PA
CBHW072111150726
47999CB00005B/2003